Dear Parent:
Your child's love of reading starts here!

Every child learns to read in a different way and at his or her own speed. Some go back and forth between reading levels and read favorite books again and again. Others read through each level in order. You can help your young reader improve and become more confident by encouraging his or her own interests and abilities. From books your child reads with you to the first books he or she reads alone, there are I Can Read Books for every stage of reading:

SHARED READING
Basic language, word repetition, and whimsical illustrations, ideal for sharing with your emergent reader

BEGINNING READING
Short sentences, familiar words, and simple concepts for children eager to read on their own

READING WITH HELP
Engaging stories, longer sentences, and language play for developing readers

READING ALONE
Complex plots, challenging vocabulary, and high-interest topics for the independent reader

ADVANCED READING
Short paragraphs, chapters, and exciting themes for the perfect bridge to chapter books

I Can Read Books have introduced children to the joy of reading since 1957. Featuring award-winning authors and illustrators and a fabulous cast of beloved characters, I Can Read Books set the standard for beginning readers.

A lifetime of discovery begins with the magical words "I Can Read!"

Visit www.icanread.com for information on enriching your child's reading experience.

JJ
O
E

Ice Age 2: Join the Pack!

Ice Age 2 The Meltdown ™ & © 2006 Twentieth Century Fox Film Corporation. All rights reserved.

Printed in the United States of America.

No part of this book may be used or reproduced in any manner whatsoever without written permission except in the case of brief quotations embodied in critical articles and reviews.

For information address HarperCollins Children's Books, a division of HarperCollins Publishers,

1350 Avenue of the Americas, New York, NY 10019.

www.icanread.com

Library of Congress catalog card number: 2005934357

ISBN-10: 0-06-083970-8—ISBN-13: 978-0-06-083970-3

❖

First Edition

I Can Read!

READING 2 WITH HELP

ICE AGE 2 ™
THE MELTDOWN

JOIN THE PACK!

Adapted by Ellie O'Ryan
Illustrations by Artful Doodlers, UK

HarperCollins*Publishers*

Meet Manny.

He is a mammoth.

He lives on an icy glacier with his pals,
Sid the sloth and Diego the
saber-toothed tiger.

Sid runs a camp at the water park—
Campo del Sid.

That means *Camp of Sid.*

"Congratulations, now you are an idiot
in two languages!" Diego tells him.

Sid wants his friends to respect him. So he decides to jump off the biggest waterslide in the park!

Diego cannot believe Sid is that dumb.

Manny grabs Sid just before he jumps.

Then Manny notices something.

The glaciers are melting!

And that can mean only one thing. . . .

A flood is coming!

Sid wants to become a water creature.

"Call me Squid," he says.

When the flood comes,

everything will be under water.

The animals must leave the

glacier—fast.

It is not safe to stay where they are.

Far away, there is a giant boat.

It will take the animals to a place

where the flood will not affect them.

All the animals pack up and leave.

Manny, Sid, and Diego leave, too.

On the trip, Manny hears bad news.

Some animals tell him that mammoths
are extinct.

Manny might be the last mammoth
in the whole world.

He sees his reflection in the icicles and
wonders if it is true.
This makes Manny feel very lonely.

Manny goes for a walk to
think things over.
Suddenly, a big tree in front of him
wobbles and shakes.
There is a mammoth hanging from it!

Manny is so glad to meet a mammoth.

Her name is Ellie.

There is just one problem.

Ellie thinks she is a possum!

These are Ellie's brothers,

Crash and Eddie.

They are possums.

Manny wonders if Ellie is a little crazy.

Manny and Ellie are the same size.

They have the same footprints.

They have the same shadows.

But Ellie still does not believe

that she is a mammoth!

Manny and his pals decide to travel
with Ellie, Crash, and Eddie.
Sid thinks Manny and Ellie are
a good pair—Ellie is lots of fun
and Manny is no fun at all!

Along the way, Manny tries to show
Ellie how to use her trunk to lift things.
Ellie does not think her trunk
works that way.
She is driving Manny nuts!

Manny and Ellie find a meadow.

Ellie remembers a time long ago.

She was alone and scared

in a meadow like this one.

A family of possums found her.

They took care of her.

Suddenly, Ellie understands—

she *is* a mammoth, after all!

"A mammoth never forgets,"

Manny says.

Ellie always knew she was different.

Now everything makes sense.

She was always bigger and stronger

than her possum friends and relatives.

Mammoths are powerful.

But they are gentle, too.

Ellie woke up thinking she was a possum.

Now she knows she is a mammoth.

The friends are almost at the boat. First, they must cross a geyser field that shoots boiling water and steam. Manny and Ellie have different ideas on how to get across.

Who will the pack follow?

Time is running out—they must choose.

"We should separate," Ellie says.

They do, and make it across safely.

But Ellie, Crash, and Eddie end up

far away from the others.

"See you at the boat!" Manny yells.

On the way to the boat,

Ellie gets trapped in a cave.

Suddenly, the big flood comes!

What will happen to Ellie?

Manny will not let Ellie down.

He has a plan to save her.

Will it work?

Manny uses the power of the water
to free Ellie.
Ellie is safe!

The mammoths swirl around
in the whirlpool.
Then the water drains out.
The big flood is over.
Manny and Ellie are safe!

Manny hears something.

It is a whole herd of mammoths!

Ellie and Manny are *not* the only

ones left.

Ellie wants to go with the mammoths.

Manny wants to stay with his pals.

But he does not want Ellie to go.

He hangs from a tree like a possum.

'Ellie, wait!" he yells.

'I want to be with you!"

Manny and Ellie do not need
to join the herd.
They can make their own herd—
with Sid, Diego, Crash, and Eddie!